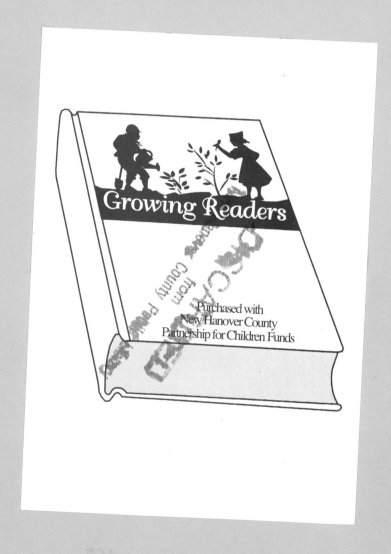

A Splendid Friend, Indeed

Suzanne Bloom

Boyds Mills Press

Text and illustrations copyright © 2005 by Suzanne Bloom

Published by Boyds Mills Press, Inc.
A Highlights Company
815 Church Street
Honesdale, Pennsylvania 18431
Printed in China

Publisher Cataloging-in-Publication Data   (U.S.)

Library of Congress Cataloging-in-Publication Data

Bloom, Suzanne, 1950–
A splendid friend, indeed / written and illustrated by Suzanne Bloom
p.   cm.
Summary: When a studious polar bear meets an inquisitive goose, they learn to be friends.
ISBN 1-59078-286-0 (alk. paper)
[1. Friendship--Fiction. 2. Individuality — Fiction. 3. Geese — Fiction. 4. Polar bear — Fiction.] I. Title.
PZ7.B6234Sp 2005   [E]—dc22
2004010780

First edition, 2005
The text is set in 42-point Optima.
The illustrations are done in pastel.
Visit our Web site at www.boydsmillspress.com

10 9 8 7 6 5 4 3 2

To R. H. B.,
my dad

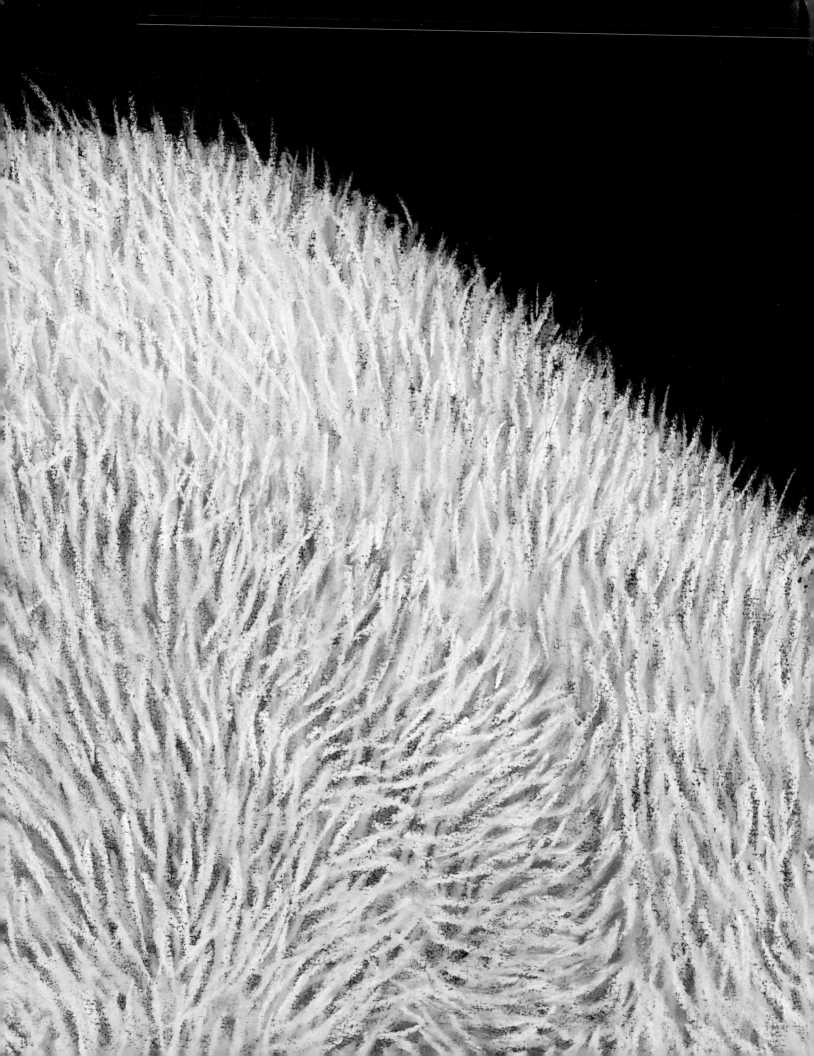

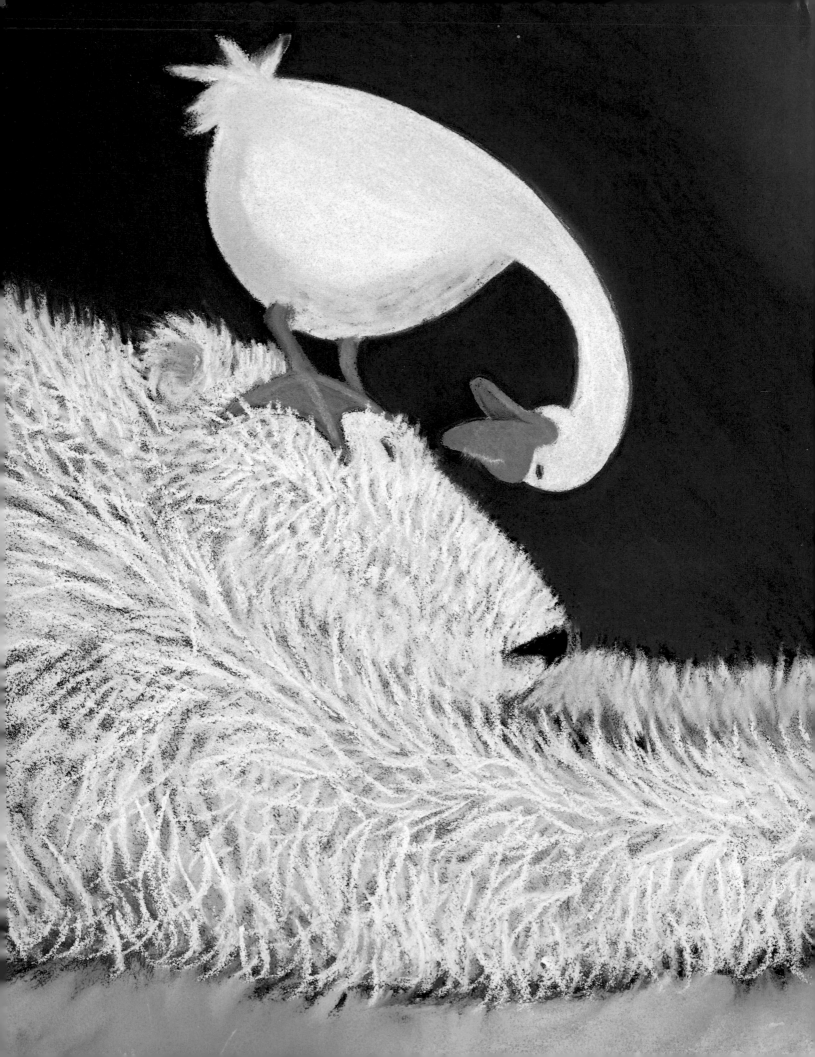

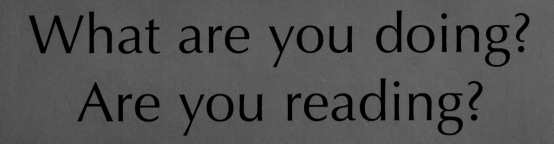

What are you doing?
Are you reading?

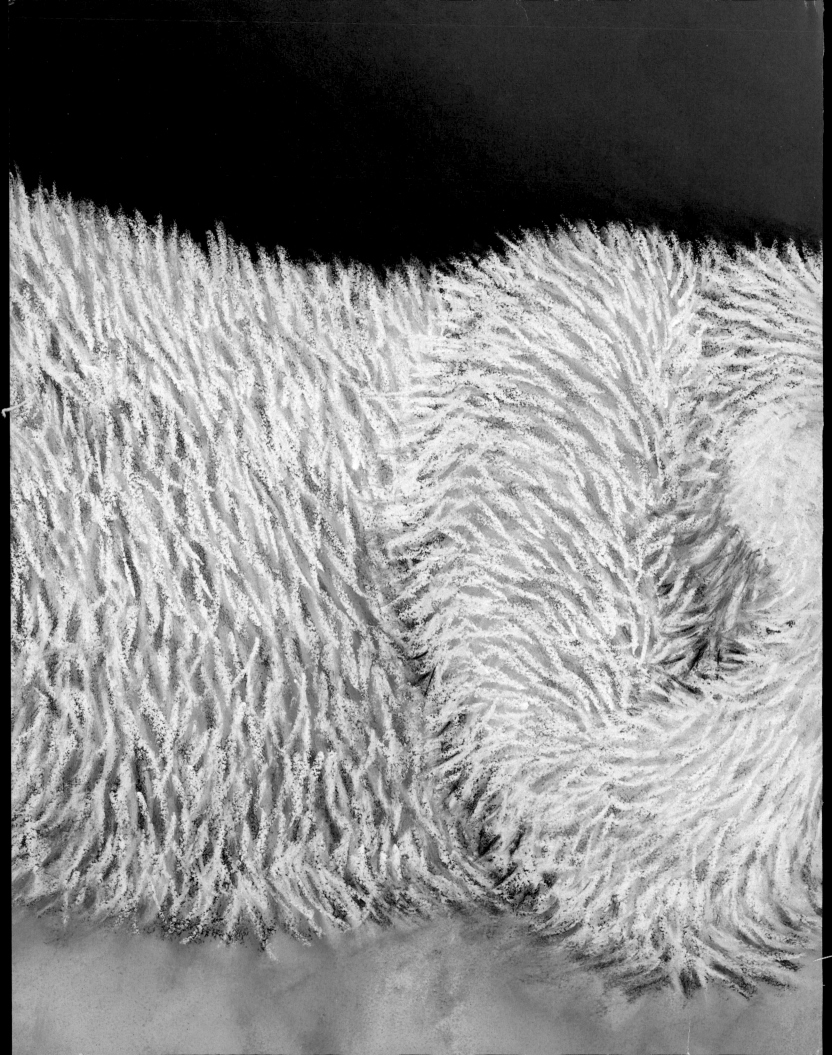

I like to read.

Do you want to hear me read?

Now what are you doing? Writing?

I like to write.

Do you want to
see me write?

What are you doing now?
Thinking?

Thinking makes me hungry.
Are you hungry?
I think I'll go make a snack.

I'm back.
I made a snack.

I wrote a note.
I'll read it to you.

I like you.
Indeed I do.
You are my splendid friend.

Thank you.
I like you, too.
Indeed, I do.

You are my splendid friend.
My splendid friend, indeed.